Bungee 70528

ANGIE BELCHER

photographs by Andy Belcher

LEARNING MEDIA®

Distributed in the United States of America by Pacific Learning,
P. O. Box 2723, Huntington Beach, CA 92647-0723
Web site: www.pacificlearning.com

Published 1999 by Learning Media Limited,
Box 3293, Wellington 6001, New Zealand
Web site: www.learningmedia.com

10 9 8 7 6 5 4

Printed in Hong Kong

ISBN 0 478 22929 1

PL 9301

"**S**amantha, phone for you," called her mom. "It's Andy. He's got a job you can help with."

Samantha rushed to the phone. "A bungee jump? A hundred and fifty feet? I don't know," she replied. "Could I bring Gemma? She's already done a bungee jump. If I get scared, maybe she'll jump instead of me."

Samantha hung up the phone. Her brother Ben was listening. "Go on, Samantha. Don't be a wimp," he teased. "It'll be a breeze – anyone can bungee jump."

"If you think it's so easy," said his mom, "why don't you go as well? Andy needs a group of children."

"No problem," said Ben, "but only if Rikki can come with me."

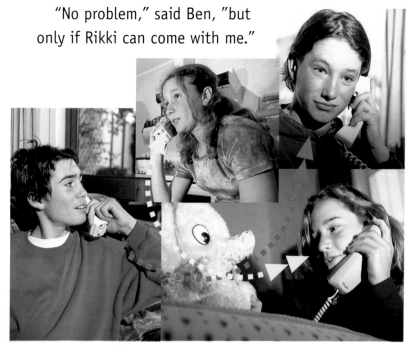

It was a long drive to the jump site, so the four friends stayed together the night before. That way they could get an early morning start. Gemma and Samantha were the first to wake up. They huddled together, talking quietly. Rikki snuggled down into his sleeping bag, hoping they'd forget about him.

Andy arrived just as the sun began to rise. "It's great bungee weather," he said cheerfully. "Did you sleep OK? I need you bright and breezy for your big day."

"I didn't sleep at all," groaned Gemma. "The bed was lumpy, and Samantha kept tossing and turning."

"You'll be all right, Gemma. You can sleep in the car on the way. C'mon, let's hit the road."

Once they were on their way, Gemma started feeling much brighter.

"It'll be so cool," she told them. "I've already done a bungee jump. It's a bit scary when you get near the edge of the platform, but once you've let go, it's OK."

"Yeah," said Ben, suddenly feeling a whole lot better. "It'll be a piece of cake."

"Good," said Samantha. "You can go first!"

Rikki just sat quietly as the car headed down the highway.

Chapter

2

As soon as the car pulled into the parking lot, everyone except Andy got out and headed for the bungee office.

"Whoa, hold on, guys!" Andy called. "We need to talk about a few things before the action starts. First, remember we're a team – a team with a job to do. We need to get some really good shots. That takes time. I want the photographs to show how exciting this sport can be. I need you to look after each other. But most of all, I want you to have a really great day. Remember, if you don't want to jump, then don't!"

Something caught Gemma's eye.

"Look!" she said. "Someone's going to jump! Let's watch."

They all ran to the viewing platform. A woman was standing at the edge of the platform. Everyone went quiet as the instructor began the countdown.

"Three, two, one – bungee!"

"Looks kind of easy," said Ben.

"Hey, that'll be you soon, Samantha," said Gemma.

"And you," Samantha replied.

"Well, maybe," said Gemma. "I've already done one."

Rikki didn't say anything.

"OK, team," said Andy. "I guess we'd better check in."

"Hi, kids. You here to jump?" asked the woman behind the counter. "I can see you're all old enough to bungee, but I have to weigh you. You have to be over ninety pounds, and the heavier you are, the shorter the rope needs to be."

"With a bit of luck, I'll be too light," Rikki whispered to Ben.

"One hundred and twenty pounds, one hundred and three, one hundred and twelve, and ninety-one. You're all OK!"

"Now," she said, "read the sign on the wall and then fill in this form."

"I can't believe I'm doing this," Ben whispered. "I'm signing a form to say that if I die, it's not their problem!"

Each of them was given a ticket, and the number was written on the back of their hand.

Andy started to get his cameras ready.

"Do you really need all that stuff?" Rikki asked.

"Sure do," said Andy. "Each camera does a different job. When you jump off the platform, I need to use an ultrawide fisheye lens to fit the jumper and lots of scenery into the picture. The camera with the motor drive takes six shots a second. That means I take a lot of pictures in the few seconds that your jump lasts.

"The zoom lens on the last camera will let me get photos of you being collected down below by the boat."

Next, one of the instructors came to meet the group. "Right, who's first?" she asked.

"Well, I've already done a jump," said Gemma, "so the others can go first."

"Well, if it was so cool, why don't you go first and show us all how it's done?" said Ben.

"Come on, guys," said Samantha. "You saw that woman jump. It doesn't look so bad. I'll go first and get it over and done with."

"Great stuff, Samantha," said Andy. "I knew I could rely on you."

Chapter 3

Samantha stepped through the rope barrier, and an instructor started to get her ready.

She wrapped thick straps around Samantha's ankles. "Feeling OK?" she asked as she began her checks. "Buckles secure, bindings tight, harness looking good. OK, we're ready to go!"

The bungee cord is like a big elastic band that's made out of 600 smaller bands.

"OK, Samantha," said the instructor. "I want you to take very small steps toward the edge of the platform. Just remember, it is really safe. You're not going to hurt yourself. When you're ready, put your arms up. Then do a really nice swan dive off the platform."

Samantha wriggled her way toward the edge. "Whoa!" she said. "It's a long way down."

"Stand nice and tall, Samantha," said the instructor. "Look straight ahead to that big tree. Take big, deep breaths. You can do it!"

Samantha felt numb. She could hear the others calling "You can do it, Samantha!"

She took a deep breath and raised her arms ...
and heard the countdown.

"Three, two, one – bungee!"

She felt the air
rushing past her
face. The ground
raced up toward
her.

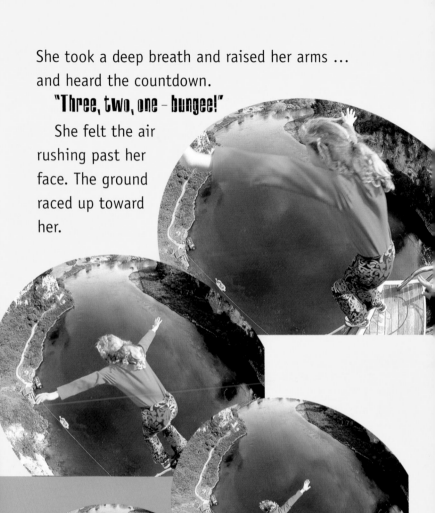

Then the cord pulled tight, and she screamed. Her body sprang back toward the top again. "Yahoo!" she screamed again and again as the elastic bungee cord bounced her up and down.

The yellow boat moved up to her. "Grab the pole!" the guides called.

She grabbed it with both hands and was lowered slowly and gently into the boat.

Chapter 4

"**G**reat stuff, Samantha. How do you feel?" they asked.

"Yeehaa! Fantastic!" she cried. A big smile stretched from ear to ear.

Up on the platform, the jump-master was talking to the other three children.

"See, Ben. A piece of cake. Just like you said. I guess you want to be next?" the instructor asked.

Ben looked around. "I think I'm going to have trouble," he said. "I don't know. It's been a bit too freaky, just waiting."

"You'll be fine," said the instructor. "Just do what Samantha did."

She ran through her check list again, and Ben shuffled toward the edge of the platform.

"Remember," she said, "don't look down. If you do, you'll just freak out. You're really brave, Ben. You can do it!"

"Three, two, one – bungee!"

Before he knew what was happening, Ben was flying through the air.

While he was still bouncing around like a yo-yo, the instructor turned toward the others. "Right. Who's next?" she asked.

"I'm not doing it now," said Gemma. "I can't. Besides, I've already done one."

"You can do it, Gemma," said Rikki. "Go on."

"I can't," said Gemma.

"Right, Rikki. Looks as if you're next," said the instructor with a large grin.

Rikki felt terrible. What would the others think if he chickened out? What if the bungee cord was worn out? What if ...?

Before he knew it, he was strapped up and standing ready to jump. He heard the others calling words of encouragement.

"Three, two, one – bungee!"

The wind rushed past, the ground rushed up, and suddenly Rikki felt great! "Yahoo!" he screamed. "Yahoo! Yahoo! Yahooooo!"

Chapter 5

Everyone gathered back on the viewing platform.

"Great work, team," said Andy. "I think I've got some awesome shots. I just need a couple more. Maybe I can get those shots when you jump, Gemma?"

"I can't," said Gemma. "I can't do it."

"Sure you can," said Ben. "We all dived and survived. It was a piece of cake!"

"Don't do it if you don't want to," said Rikki.

"I just don't think I can bring myself to walk to the edge of that platform. If I had someone with me, then maybe it would feel different."

"Hey, that's not a problem," said the instructor. "You can do a tandem jump – the two of you linked together. Now, who wants to do another jump?"

"Pass!" said Ben and Rikki.

"OK," said Samantha, "I'll jump with you. It'll be awesome. Tell you what – let's do it backwards. Then we won't even have to look down."

The instructor attached leg wraps to each of them and then joined the two sets of leg straps together. The two girls moved toward the end of the platform.

"Now, watch out you don't bang your heads together, and don't grab hold of the cord on the way down. Are you ready?"

"Ready," said the girls.

"Three, two, one – bungee!"

Screams echoed around the cliffs, bounced off the water, and rose through the air toward the boys above.

"Yahoo!" the girls screamed ... and screamed ... and screamed.

"We did it. We all did it!" the boys yelled down to them.

"What a team," said Andy. "Mission completed!"

Back at the top, each of the four excited friends got a Certificate of Courage and a piece of bungee cord as a souvenir.

"This certificate is special," said Samantha. "It's for our tandem jump – Bungee 70528!"

CERTIFICATE of Courage

Samantha Weidmann & Gemma Munroe

For becoming heroes of the Order of Bungee Adventurers, by expertly performing a daring leap of 154 feet from "The Plank" over the mighty Waikato River.

This award is conferred with the unanimous approval and congratulations of the Bungee Team.

BUNGEE 70528